P9-DOA-700

As the Crow Flies

DISCARDED

For Jason,
two seconds as the heart beats
—E. W.

For Aiden Fishbein and his dad Bruce Bayly,
a model pair
—J. S.

Clarion Books
a Houghton Mifflin Company imprint
215 Park Avenue South, New York, NY 10003
Text copyright © 1998 by Elizabeth Winthrop
Illustrations copyright © 1998 by Joan Sandin
Illustrations executed in watercolor and pencil.
Type is 15/21 Sabon. Book design by Carol Goldenberg.

All rights reserved.
For information about permission to reproduce selections from this book, write to
Permissions, Houghton Mifflin Company,
215 Park Avenue South, New York, NY 10003.
Printed in the USA

Library of Congress Cataloging-in-Publication Data

Winthrop, Elizabeth.
As the crow flies / by Elizabeth Winthrop ; illustrated by Joan Sandin.
   p.   cm.
Summary: A second-grader describes how he feels when his father comes all the way from Delaware to Arizona to spend a week with him.
ISBN 0-395-77612-0
[1. Fathers and sons—Fiction. 2. Divorce—Fiction.] I. Sandin, Joan, ill. II. Title.
PZ7.W768Arx   1997
[Fic]—dc21   97-10446
CIP   AC

HOR 10 9 8 7 6 5 4 3 2 1

As the Crow Flies

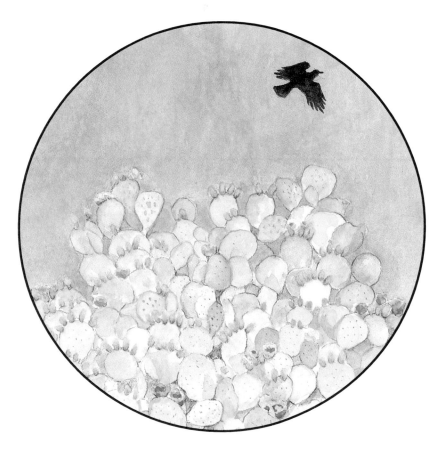

by Elizabeth Winthrop
illustrated by Joan Sandin

CLARION BOOKS

New York

NEW HANOVER COUNTY
PUBLIC LIBRARY
201 CHESTNUT STREET
WILMINGTON, N C 28401

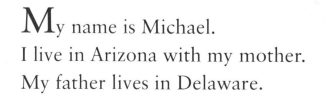

My name is Michael.
I live in Arizona with my mother.
My father lives in Delaware.

My mother and father don't speak to each other
except when they have to make plans about me.
I love my mother and my father.
I hate the way they don't speak to each other
anymore.

"How far away are you?"
I ask my father
when he calls on the phone.
"About two thousand miles," he says.
"That's far," I say.
"Seven states as the crow flies," he says,
"two seconds as the heart beats."

Once a year
my father comes to Arizona to see me.
He takes a room in a motel
and I stay with him for a week.

The day my father comes
I can't listen to anything the teacher is saying.
I jump around in my seat.
I look at the clock a hundred times an hour.
My teacher understands.
She sends me to run errands.

"We need more paper towels in the boys' bathroom,"
I say to Mr. Wilson, the custodian. "My father's
coming all the way from Delaware to see me today."
"Wow," Mr. Wilson says. "That's a long way."
"Seven states as the crow flies," I say.

Finally the bell rings for dismissal.
I run out the door.
There's my father waiting for me.
He grabs me and we hug
and he pounds me on the back
and I pound him on the back.
He carries my duffel bag out to the car
he's rented for the week.
"So, buddy, what do you think of this one?" he asks.
I walk around the car and kick the tires.
"I like it," I say. "Blue is my favorite color."
Then we get inside
and I roll the windows up and down
and I punch all the radio buttons.

In the motel
our room has two big beds and a TV
and a table with two chairs
where I can do my homework.
In the bathroom
there are little bars of soap
all wrapped up like presents
and little bottles of shampoo
and a shower cap in a plastic envelope.
I put the shower cap in my duffel bag
to take home to my mother.

"Here we are, Mikey," my father says.
"Home sweet home."
He gets out the books he wants to read to me
and the new puzzles and the games we can
play together
and the photo albums from before,
because I like to look at pictures of myself
when I was small enough
to sit up on his shoulders.

Every day we get up
and eat breakfast in the coffee shop
and the waitress gives me an extra doughnut.
I don't have to take the bus to school
because my father drives me in the car.
Every afternoon, when school is over,
he comes to pick me up.

We go shopping
or we go hiking
or we walk up and down the streets
and look in the store windows.

If it's raining,
we go back to the motel
and watch TV
and play games until dinner.
We eat in a different restaurant every night
because that makes it more interesting.

After dinner
I do my homework,
and my father helps me,
and then he makes me take a bath
and then I go to bed.

I lie in the bed and look at the funny bumps
on the ceiling.
On the ceiling in my room
my mother pasted stars and moons
that glow in the dark.
I miss my bed at home.
I miss my pet turtle, B.J.
I hope my mother is feeding him.
I miss my bike and the rides I take with my friend Jake.
I am sick of missing people.
When my father is in Delaware, I miss him.
Right now he is reading in his bed.
He has a little light hooked on to the top of the book
so he won't keep me awake.
"Are you asleep, Mikey?" my father asks.
"No," I say.
"What are you thinking about?" he asks.
"Nothing," I say. I don't want to tell him.
"Want to call your mom?" he asks.
"Yes," I say. "I have to tell her to feed B.J."
"Good idea."

He brings the phone over to my bed
and then goes into the bathroom.

Mom says that B.J. is fine, but he misses me,
and Jake is waiting to go biking with me.
I hang up the phone
and pull the covers right up to my chin
and wait for Dad to come out of the bathroom
and kiss me good night.

On the last day of my father's visit
I take him to see my teacher after school.
She gets out my folder
and shows him the papers I've written
and my spelling tests
and the pictures I've drawn.
I show him the books we've been reading
and the ant farm for science
and the music corner.
"Michael loves to play the recorder," my teacher says.
"He's very musical."
"When I was his age, I played the drums,"
my father says.
"You never told me that before," I say.

Suddenly I am sad.
Tomorrow morning my father will drive me to school
and then he will go straight to the airport
and fly back across seven states to Delaware.
It is raining outside.
I don't want to go to the motel and watch TV
and play the same games over again.
"Mrs. Stengel," I say,
"can Dad and I stay here this afternoon?
I want to show him more things."
She looks at my father.
He smiles.
"Sure," she says.

I make my father sit in one of the little chairs
and I read him my favorite book about the crocodile.
I give him a spelling test
with all the hard words from the book
like *bathroom* and *belongings*.
He stares at the ceiling
and rolls the pencil back and forth with his fingers
just the way I do.
When he's done,
I mark up his test with a big red marker.
"One hundred percent!
You're very smart, Dad," I say.
"Even if you're too old for the second grade."
He laughs and laughs.
Then I play him the last three songs
I learned on the recorder.
"Play them again," he says,
and he beats time on the drum.

Mr. Wilson knocks on the door.
"This is my father," I yell
over the noise of the drum.
My father lifts one hand and waves,
but keeps on drumming with the other.
"This looks like fun," Mr. Wilson says.
He turns his bucket over
and beats out the rhythm
with two big red markers.
We make a great band.
"It's getting late," Mr. Wilson says.
"I'd better mop that back hall
before I close up."

"I'm hungry," I say.
"Me too," says my father.
So we put away the books
and the red markers and the instruments
and say good night to Mr. Wilson.

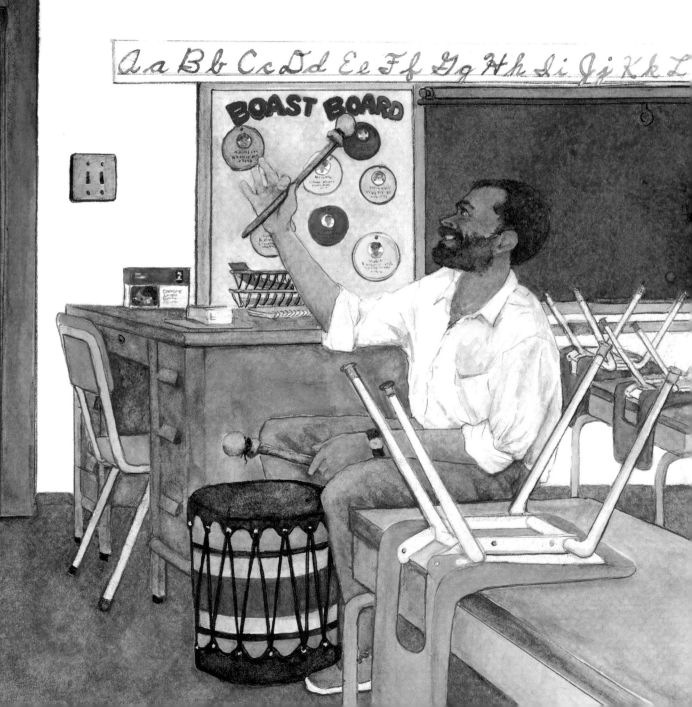

The next morning at breakfast
I don't feel like eating.
My father wraps my two doughnuts
in a napkin and puts them in my lunch box.
"I have a surprise for you," he says.
"I talked to your mom on the phone last night.
We both think you're old enough
to come visit me this summer."
I stare at him.
"All the way to Delaware in an airplane?"
I say. "Across seven states?"
"Two thousand miles as the crow flies,"
my father says.
He drives me to school
and I roll the windows up and down
and I punch the buttons on the radio.
I wish it would make the car go slower,
but it doesn't.

When we get to school,
my father gives me my duffel bag
and my lunch box
and he hugs me long and hard
and pounds me on the back.
"Remember, Mikey," he says,
"two seconds as the heart beats."
And I nod yes.

When I get home
I'm going biking with my friend Jake.
I can't wait to tell him
that I'm going to take an airplane
and fly across seven states to Delaware all by myself.
Two thousand miles as the crow flies.
I bet Jake's never even been on an airplane.

NEW HANOVER COUNTY PUBLIC LIB.

3 4200 00484 1926

DISCARDED

6/98

NEW HANOVER COUNTY PUBLIC LIBRARY
201 Chestnut Street
Wilmington, N.C. 28401

GAYLORD S